Harriet,
You'll Drive Me Wild!

BY MEM FOX

ILLUSTRATED BY MARLA FRAZEE

SCHOLASTIC INC.

New York Toronto London Auckland Sydney
Mexico City New Delhi Hong Kong Buenos Aires

To Wendy Bean, the Soft-Voice Queen
— M E M   F O X

To my sister, Janel—transplendent amidst the Legos
— M A R L A   F R A Z E E

ISBN 0-439-30554-3

Text copyright © 2000 by Mem Fox.
Illustrations copyright © 2000 by Marla Frazee.
All rights reserved.
Published by Scholastic Inc., 555 Broadway, New York, NY 10012,
by arrangement with Harcourt, Inc.
SCHOLASTIC and associated logos are trademarks and/or
registered trademarks of Scholastic Inc.

12 11 10 9   3 4 5 6/0

Printed in the U.S.A.   40

First Scholastic printing, September 2001

The illustrations in this book were done in pencil and transparent drawing inks
on Strathmore paper, hot press finish.
The display type was set in Minion Swash italic.
The text type was set in Adobe Caslon.
Designed by Kaelin Chappell and Marla Frazee.

Harriet Harris was a pesky child.
She didn't mean to be. She just was.

One morning at breakfast, she knocked over
a glass of juice, just like that.

Her mother didn't like to yell, so instead she said,
"Harriet, my *darling* child."
"I'm sorry," said Harriet, and she was.

At snacktime, she dribbled jam all over her jeans, just like that.

Her mother didn't like to yell, so instead she said,
"Harriet, my *darling* child. Harriet, you'll drive me wild."
"I'm sorry," said Harriet, and she was.

Before lunch, when Harriet was painting a picture, she dripped paint onto the carpet, just like that.

Her mother didn't like to yell, so instead she said,
"Harriet, my *darling* child. Harriet, you'll drive me wild.
Harriet, sweetheart, what are we to do?"
"I'm sorry," said Harriet, and she was.

At lunch, Harriet slid off her chair and the tablecloth came with her, just like that.

Her mother didn't like to yell, so instead she said,

"Harriet, my *darling* child. Harriet, you'll drive me wild.

Harriet, sweetheart, what are we to do?

Harriet Harris, I'm talking to *you*."

"I'm sorry," said Harriet, and she was.

Later that afternoon, when Harriet was meant to be
napping, she ripped open a pillow, just like that.

A thousand feathers flew in every direction.

There was a terrible silence.

Then Harriet's mother began to yell.
She yelled and yelled and yelled.

"I'm sorry," Harriet cried. "I'm really, really sorry."

*H*er mother took a deep breath.

"I know you are," she said, hugging Harriet tight.

"I'm sorry, too. I shouldn't have yelled, and I wish I hadn't.

But sometimes it happens, just like that."

"Big mess," said Harriet.
"A *very* big mess," said her mother.
And she started to laugh.

*A*nd they laughed and laughed and went on laughing
as they picked up the feathers together.